The Ministry

Colin Anderson

Ukiyoto Publishing

All global publishing rights are held by

Ukiyoto Publishing

Published in 2023

ISBN 9789357709279

Content Copyright © Colin Anderson

All rights reserved.

No part of this publication may be reproduced, transmitted, or stored in a retrieval system, in any form by any means, electronic, mechanical, photocopying, recording or otherwise, without the prior permission of the publisher.

The moral rights of the author have been asserted.

This is a work of fiction. Names, characters, businesses, places, events, locales, and incidents are either the products of the author's imagination or used in a fictitious manner. Any resemblance to actual persons, living or dead, or actual events is purely coincidental.

This book is sold subject to the condition that it shall not by way of trade or otherwise, be lent, resold, hired out or otherwise circulated, without the publisher's prior consent, in any form of binding or cover other than that in which it is published.

Contents

Prologue	1
Bad Situation	4
A New Home	7
Consequences...	12
New Opportunities	16
New Recruit	20
A Lease On Life	23
Retaliation	28
New & Improved	34
Showdown	40

Prologue

"Within a dystopian city, lies the secret covert organisation "The Ministry", governing all with an iron fist and a ever endless watching eye. They're greedy hand controlling everything. If you default on your payments, they send someone to... collect!"

We are following a silhouette of a woman, swaying her hips seductively as she heads straight into a dive bar called Mac's. She walks over to a vacant table and sits down, puts her feet up onto the table. We see she is part human, part cyborg, twirling her gun in and out of its holster. The owner walks over to her.

Mac:

You've got some fucking nerve walking back in here.

Woman:

(Seductively)

Mac, surely we can... sort this out!

Mac:

Nice try! Now pay your tab.... bitch!

Woman:

You get paid, when I get my money.

Mac reveals a sawn off shot gun, slightly moving it. She catches it in her cybernetic eye.

Mac:

I don't wanna use this kid!

2   The Ministry

The woman moves fluidly and swiftly, grabs him by the neck, pushing the gun barrel of her pistol into his head.
Woman (Softly) :
Like I said, you get paid when I do. Now be a good little slut, and say my name!
Mac :
Nikita....
Nikita :
Wrong answer! Try again... or the next fucking thing you see, is your brains decorating the walls.
Mac :
Si... silent knight.
Nikita :
Good boy, now fuck off!
She lets him go, rubbing his neck reflexively. She shows off her gun skills by twirling her pistol cowboy style, as she easily puts it in the holster. The other patrons just stare, she winks at them and blows a kiss as she sits back down. A man dressed in a suit joins her, putting a drink down on the table.
Man :
The ministry needs your services.
Nikita :
Who's fallen behind?
Man :
William Reed, he is late on his payment... Uploading details to you now.
Nikita :
Got em.
Man :
Reimbursement on completion.

The man walks away, her cybernetic legs whinge into life as she stands seductively and heads out. She gets on her impressive styled bike nicknamed, Moon light, it starts up and the powerful engine gives passers-by a fright. We watch as she rides off into the distance....

4

Bad Situation

Nikita climbs off her bike, turns and rushes to the wall of the security gate. She quickly briefly looks at the huge mansion before her. She scans with her cybernetic eye, to find the easiest route. She easily leaps over the wall, lands softly and runs to avoid the cameras and effortlessly makes her way inside, she heads upstairs stealthily, passing a little boys bedroom who is sound asleep to the master bedroom. A dim light shines from the slight gap from the door, she gently pushes the door, it creaks as it does. William knows what's about to happen. He sits in a black leather chair, his hands clasped together, waiting on her.

William Reed
Do come in my dear. Take a seat, please.
Nikita
I'm not here to make nice, fuck face.
William Reed
Isn't it customary to grant the condemned, one final request?
Nikita
(Frustrated Sigh)
Fine.
She sits down in a similar chair.
William Reed

I appreciate your courtesy. I know why they sent you!
Nikita
You ain't a dumb shit after all!
William Reed
You will get the payment, also I will die... no doubt about that, but what if there was another way... to walk a... different path. To start anew... far from the ministry's peering gaze
Nikita
You want me to walk away, say fuck you? Nobody can simply just... leave
William Reed
You can... silent knight. But only if you truly want this. I offer a way out... To strike at their black heart.
Nikita
I.... can't.
William Reed
You can... this program I'm uploading. It will... keep you under there radar. A new lease on life.
William stands up, walks over to his night stand, picks up a copy of her gun and cybernetic hand, which he switches his hand to.
Nikita
What... the fuck?
William Reed
As you can see, I am fully prepared for this scenario. Payment is now complete. Once I am dead, the program will activate. It will constantly scramble your exact location... Farewell... silent knight...
William puts the gun under his chin, he pulls the trigger. Skull and brain matter fly every where. Blood

pouring out his nose as he slumps to the floor. Nikita stands in utter silence and shock. A computer voice is faintly heard saying " payment pending"

A white flash is seen, and we are back in macs dive bar. Nikita stares blankly into space, going over what just happened. The CEO of the ministry sits down, rousing her from the deep thoughts swirling in her mind.

CEO Vandenberg

Congratulations on a job well done, silent knight. The thorn in our side is no longer an irritant. We can now recoup our losses.

Nikita

What about the boy, he'll be homeless.

CEO Vandenberg

That's no concern to me. Collateral damage.

Nikita

And the house

CEO Vandenberg

Added bonus for being efficient.... rest up for a while, I'll contact you for the next assignment.

<u>End of Chapter One</u>

A New Home

Several weeks have passed since, to Nikita what seemed to be a failure. Fortunately the boy was picked up by his grandparents before she moved in. She stands at the work station, staring into the mirror. Thoughts run wild in her head, shaking off the cobwebs she returns to rebuilding her new gun. It is a futuristic version of a desert Eagle. Her hands are a blur as its reassembled, she catches her reflection in the glass door heading to the living room, rotating her left shoulder, slightly exposing her steel arm components, as she holsters the gun.

Nikita
(To Herself)
I gotta get this fixed...
Her internal com systems crackles as someone tries to reach her.
Voice :
H….ello is… Nikita? Come to… coordinates sent.
Nikita :
(Frustrated)
Damn it!
She exits her repair station, heading to the main door. But another voice catches her off guard. She turns to see another female cyborg.
Woman :
Going somewhere?
Nikita :

What do you want... Razor!

Razor:

Your not thinking of walking away, are you? Be a shame to cut you down in your... prime.

Razor stifles her laughter. Nikita glares at razor in pure anger, but holds back.

Nikita:

(Fake Shock)

As if I would.

Razor:

(Angrily)

Cut the shit! The ministry sent me, to find you. They.... somehow can't locate you. Curious, isn't it!

Nikita:

I'm only following orders, to relax!

Razor:

NOT THIS LONG. I'VE HAD TO CLEAN UP YOUR FUCKING SHIT.

Nikita:

(Coldly)

About time you got off your fat lazy ass.

Razor rushes to grab Nikita, who is not quick enough to defend herself. She slams her violently hard against the wall, which forces her head into it. She stares psychotically at Nikita smiling.

Razor:

(Eerily Sweet)

You believe your better than me? Your old... obsolete. There's a new generation rising up the ranks. Everyone knows your top dog. Even our glorious benefactor thinks the sun shines out your ass.

Nikita slams her knee into razors stomach hard, then flings her over her shoulder. Razor crashes into a coffee table instantly breaking it. Nikita casually sits on top of her, pushing the gun barrel very hard into her head.

Nikita :

(Softly)

Ahhh... the cockiness of the loud mouth. Driven by there ego not to mention brash. You see... the difference is, I don't have to brag about my... skills. Makes you sloppy... slow to react. I could... splatter your brains everywhere but, consider this a one time pass.... now fuck off!

She gets off razor and helps her up, who scowls in return. Nikita places her gun back in its holster, nods to razor to go. She storms out, answering her com link. She rolls her eyes in relief, she heads to her laptop, sits on the sofa and opens it up, and inputs the coordinates she received. They reveal an old rundown factory in the industrial sector.

Nikita :

(Chuckles Slightly)

Heavily guarded, tight security check points. I'm good.. but I'm not that good.

The computer voice faintly announces " clearance level 1"

Nikita :

Well, that answers that question

***

Hours later, Nikita zooms by on moon light, the sun fades quickly as the night takes over. We see a very large industrial complex coming in to view. She slows to a stop, approaching a check point. The guard gives her a quick glance. His screen illuminates his face. The barrier lifts and she slowly drives away, then speeds up as she heads to her destination.

After a brief drive she finds herself outside the factory, climbing off her bike and scanning the building. But there's heavy interference which is messing up her scans. She gives up and heads on in, drawing her gun in a defensive position.

Once inside she steps slowly, the only light we see is the light from her eyes. Suddenly the lights flick on, to reveal William Reed with two other men, sitting there in a professional manner. Nikita is confused. He gestures to her to sit, which she does.

Nikita:

What the shit?

William Reed:

To see a dead man alive? A clone, if you must ask... I have many. I can assure you, I am the real William Reed.

Nikita:

I saw you blow your fucking brains, all over your walls.

William Reed:

So the plan was a success. I had to make them feel, that they'd won... my company was a significant threat to there conglomerate. Intimidation doesn't frighten me I'm afraid. So instead they sent you.

Nikita:

This really makes no fucking sense, why would they be afraid of you!

William Reed:

Because... my dear... I am a VERY powerful wealthy man. My business easily outmatches them. My proposal is, join me... be on the winning team. We strive to make this city profitable.
Nikita :
I .... can't. If... I leave, I'm screwed. They'd try to kill me, every damn fucking day.
William Reed :
I agree, the... dampening protocol was in its infancy. But we have improved its functionality. Also we can improve on your implants.
Nikita :
Can you promise I'll be safe?
William Reed :
As Fort Knox.

<u>End of Chapter Two</u>

Consequences...

Razor is standing within a very large hall, bronze in colour. The members of the ministry sit in very comfortable recliners, Vandenberg sits in a blood red coloured recliner. He looks at her with distain. He dismisses the others and there image shimmers then disappears.

Director Vandenberg
Report!
Razor
I found her, she's in the safe house.
Director Vandenberg
And did you handle it?
Razor
I....
Director Vandenberg
Clearly, you let her slip through your fingers.
Razor
(Angry)
Bullshit, she got the jump on me!
Director Vandenberg
 YOU WERE SLOPPY!
Razor :
(Softly)
I wasn't sloppy...
Director Vandenberg :

Save your pathetic attempts to justify your actions. I think you are not fit for purpose. Since I'm in a... generous mood... I'll give you one final chance. DONT disappoint me.

He dismisses her. She heads to a nearby elevator. Which takes her to a repair centre. She storms out the elevator, up to a work station and slams her fists down hard in anger and frustration. A service android named Katie shuffles up to her, placing a reassuring hand on her shoulder.

Katie :

Don't take it personally. There obviously jealous, of your talents. I've gone over the information you provided! Unfortunately I wasn't to able to find anything significant, but I did discover something... unusual

Razor :

Do tell!

Katie :

I found a... primitive... cloaking energy signature , its weak but I believe I cam locate it

Razor :

Can you pinpoint its location?

Katie :

It will take some time.

***

Director Vandenberg is standing in front of the founding members within there grand hall. It is decorated with gold walls, recesses within the wall are copper busts of the members.

Director Vandenberg :

The Ministry

I've called for this meeting, to put forward my proposal to unleash our... newest recruit.
Member 1
That... is not for you to decide... Vandenberg
Director Vandenberg
Razor is not living up to standards. She had failed to locate silent knight.
Member 2
Indeed, but according to sources... you have given her one more chance.
Member 3
We've given you clearance to access our resources. Inform this... razor... that she has our... gratitude.
Member 4
Don't fail us, Vandenberg.

He bows slightly then heads for the exit. A short car ride later he is back in his own building. He calls to Razor who comes from the repair bay.
Razor
You called?
Director Vandenberg
You don't answer to me anymore. So... your no longer my problem. If you fuck up, its all on you.
Razor :
So... I have unlimited access to there... Ooooh
She runs off to the repair bay excitedly. He sulks off to his study and he locks the door. He sits in his chair, pours himself a whisky. Swirling the glass, plotting.
Director Vandenberg :
(To Himself)

These old fucking dicks, don't know who there dealing with. Giving that useless bitch, there unlimited resources. Computer? Display my... private project.
Computer Voice :
Understood.
Director Vandenberg :
From this moment on all data is to be secured on my private server
Computer Voice :
Yes sir, Mr Vandenberg.

<u>End of Chapter Three</u>

New Opportunities

We follow Nikita and William as they take a tour of the modest sized building. It is very highly technology advanced. They enter one of the many rooms. It is a research and development room. A male scientist makes his appearance.
William Reed:
Ahhh, Dr. Wagner so glad to see you. I would like you to meet...
Dr. Wagner:
Nikita, I've read your files.
Nikita:
(Ironically)
Nice to meet you too, doc!
Dr. Wagner:
Doctor, if you please! Mr Reed has informed me.
William Reed:
I'll let you both get better acquainted
William leaves the room as they both glare at each other.
Dr. Wagner:
I see your the new candidate.
Nikita:
I'm... not sure yet.
Dr. Wagner:

Listen to me, I know all about the ministry. Not an easy to, up and leave. Trust me... I know.
He pulls down his shirt collar to reveal a barcode like tattoo.
Nikita :
You were, like me?
Dr. Wagner :
I was.... my call sign was... Panther. Silent and deadly. They had recently recruited you, so eager to make a name for yourself. Not to mention the money.
Nikita :
True, the thrills of all of it... was awesome in the beginning.... even making the big bucks was cool.... but now, its like....
Dr. Wagner :
Repetitive? I myself went through the same thoughts. It was then I had a chance meeting with Mr Reed. He showed me a more, better way to live a more... productive life.
Nikita :
I....
Dr. Wagner :
Your still not sure, are you? I understand your apprehension... but this is the better option. For once, I can actually contribute to society ... rather than taking from it.
Nikita :
I best get back...
She heads towards the door, but is stopped my William.
William Reed :

Leaving us so soon? Let me show something, before you do.

They both leave the room and head towards Williams rather impressive office. It is decked out with modest paintings and furniture. Nikita sits on a silk comfortable sofa. William doesn't sit but looks out the window.

Nikita :

So... what do you want to show me.

William Reed :

(Sighs Remorsefully)

Back then I was a young member of the ministry. But there dubious ways... was a concern to me. I made my opinion very clear, but I was shunned. The rest they say, is history.

Nikita :

So... how do I join?

William Reed :

You already have. I will personally oversee your repairs. I will inform Dr. Wagner of the necessary arrangements. I will personally pay your expenses , welcome to... Safeguard.

Moments later we see Nikita step out of the research centre, repaired and in a new sleek body. It is black in appearance but it is a dark purple. She twirls her upgraded gun, then back into its holster

William Reed :

You've outdone yourself, my old friend. I think you deserve a raise.

Dr. Wagner :

That won't be necessary my friend, your thanks is payment enough. How do you feel my dear?

Nikita :
(Seductively)
So good... I'd fuck myself. Nice going doctor, I'll certainly... repay you.
Dr. Wagner :
(Chuckles)
I appreciate the offer, but I'm gay.
***

Vandenberg is overlooking a holographic projection of his secret project. Taking out doesn't like, placing in what he does. He smiles at the finished image.
Director Vandenberg :
Excellent, all I need is a willing subject
Computer Voice :
Sir, if I may. I have a suitable candidate
Director Vandenberg :
Who?
Computer Voice :
He's a nobody, constantly a problem for authorities. Shall I... recruit him?
Director Vandenberg :
Please do, let's see if this one is more... compatible.

<u>End of Chapter Four</u>

New Recruit

Inside the local police station, sits Dillon. A unknown local thug. He sits cuffed to the seat inside the jail cell bored. He wears a brown worn leather coat, patch over his right eye, his left eye is slightly milky white, olive skin and black beard. A officer comes up and opens the cell, nods to him he's free to go. Once outside, a limousine is waiting for him. After a brief drive, we watch as he heads inside the ministry's building.
He makes his way to the main hall, where Vandenberg is waiting on him, he gets up to greet him, smiling.
Director Vandenberg:
Mr Carter, pleasure to meet you.
Dillon Carter:
(Gruff Tone)
Whatever dip shit, what you want?
Director Vandenberg:
An golden opportunity... be your own boss.
Dillon Carter:
(Laughs)
Your fucking crazy man, even I wouldn't take on my employers.
Director Vandenberg:
What if you could? I can supply everything, it may involve some... surgery... but it will be worth it. Not to mention the possibility to make big bucks.

Several hours later, we see metallic feet step out the research room. He is now a cyborg, dark red in colour. He easily twirls his twin guns between his fingers then back in there holster.
Dillon Carter :
(Slight Metallic Tone)
Nice! So... what now.
Director Vandenberg :
Your new call sign is... Tracker. I've given you the most excellent of upgrades. Oh... one more thing, you go rogue, I'll detonate the miniature bomb implanted. Play by the rules and you'll be handsomely rewarded.
Tracker :
Got it... boss! Who's needing fucked up.
Director Vandenberg :
Well, you'll need a safe house. Your old employers home should suffice. Now that you have the tools, I'm sure it will be not a problem. Your next agenda will be to... eliminate the competition. I mean... they used you to fatten there own pockets... leaving you penniless.

Trackers fists clench in anger. He turns and heads out the building. Vandenberg smiles and chuckles. A few hours later, tracker is on a nearby rooftop scouting a local nightclub. He knows who owns it, watching as his old boss stumbles out drunk and into an awaiting car. Tracker follows on foot, easily vaulting over the rooftops. The car enters a brass security gate, and stops at a extravagant house.

He waits patiently, picking his moment. Once the gate closes he makes his move. Moving parkour style over the wall, landing stealthily. He quickly calculates the easiest route, running towards the house, dodging the lonely guard making his rounds.

Tracker eventually makes his way inside, looking for his target. To his surprise another three of his employers are here. He makes his way into the dining room, announcing his presence.

Tracker:

I'm touched... convenient of you bringing your friends... Mason...

Mason:

The freak show, is down the street pal!

They all laugh, not noticing a gun at his head. Once they all notice it there is silence.

Tracker:

Not laughing now are we, fuck boy!

Mason

That voice... YOU!

Tracker smiles psychotically then pulls the trigger. Before the others react, he kills them too. He chuckles a little then holsters his guns. He taps his head to activate his internal com system.

Tracker:

It's done, there all dead... the other three were already here. Thanks boss...

He hangs up, laughing a little. He pushes masons corpse of the comfy seat and relaxes, putting his feet on the now blood stained table. He uses his coms system to call out a clean up crew.

End of Chapter Five

A Lease On Life

Nikita is admiring herself in the mirror, her face and body repaired, now sleek and figure hugging, light sapphire in colour. William stands behind her smiling.

William Reed:

What do you think?

Nikita:

I like it, thanks

William Reed:

No need my dear, Dr. Wagner improved your implants. Not to mention a flexible spinal cord. Feel free to do a systems check.

Nikita reads her heads up display, shocked at what she sees.

Nikita:

I'm... blown away with what you and the good doctor did. What's this... adaptive armour?

Dr. Wagner:

Ahhh, my latest project. If physically attacked... the force of impact is distributed, to cause less damage. If the attack repeats then your armour... learns and lessens the damage more. Your targeting system is more... defined. Not to mention you can now see in all spectres. Finally if you stay still, your stealth mode will activate. Making you invisible.

The Ministry

William Reed :

I asked the good doctor to add that, a token of my gratitude. Also your codename will remain, remember it is now for the greater good.

Nikita :

No... that... person is dead... call me... White Mist.

Her body colour changes to a bright white, her eyes change colour to a bright rose.

William Reed :

If you are overwhelmed, just say safeguard. And our transporters will lock on to your location, then bring you home.

Nikita :

Thanks, I'll keep that in mind.

***

Many hours later, Nikita lounges on the rooftop of Macs bar, sipping a cold beer. She occasionally glances at the ministry's building, she spits out the mouthful of beer and scrambles to her feet as one of the members makes his way onto the street. Her cybernetic eye zooms in to get a closer look.

Nikita :

I have eyes on a walking corpse.

William answers via a com link.

William Reed :

Not the time to crack jokes, white mist. Where's he headed?

Nikita :

That stuffy boys club.

William Reed :

Literally... members only, this could be a problem.

Nikita :

(Coyly)
I know of... one way to get in.
Her appearance changes to a more exotic one and hides her cybernetics, with a revealing dress with high heels, accentuated alluring makeup. She sways her hips as she walks to the entrance. A bouncer stops her.
Bouncer:
Sorry lady, members only
Nikita:
I'm sure you could make a...exemption.
He is unfazed. The member known as Falcon, hears the commotion outside and investigates. He spots Nikita. He smiles happily, trying to remain calm.
Falcon:
What seems to be the trouble?
Bouncer:
She's not a member sir.
Falcon:
Come now! Well... my dear, what do we owe the pleasure?
Nikita:
(Shyly)
I was looking for a good time, but there's only dive bars. I want to go somewhere... sophisticated.
Mingle with people with more class.
Falcon:
Oh we can... accommodate you, my dear. Come... let me get you out of the cold.
The two head inside, as Falcon glances angrily at the bouncer. Once inside they walk through the beautifully decorated silk blue walls, exotic dancers are seen taking

there turn on stage, taking drinks to tables that have little lamps on them. They head to his private room, locking the door and sits beside her, leering over her.
Nikita :
(Fake Laughing)
Someone's horny!
Falcon :
I maybe a bit old, but I know how to give a slut like you... a good fucking.
Nikita let's him slobber on her neck, as she quickly scans for cameras. None are found, then pushes him off.

Nikita :

Easy tiger, we have plenty of time for that.
Falcon strips naked and slowly moves towards her. She smiles as she pretends to undress but stealthily retrieves her gun. Changing its setting to silent and aims it at him , locking on to his vital organs. She reveals her true self.
Falcon :
What's the meaning of this.
Nikita :
Surprise bitch! You REALLY thought, I'd fuck... YOU? Look at your old wrinkly ass, with your tiny pecker. I'm here to deliver a message....
Falcon :
Threats don't intimidate me... girly!
Nikita shoots him in his kneecaps. Falcons legs instantly buckle and he falls to the floor, blood oozing out his open wounds. He tries to control the agonising pain surging through his body.
Nikita :

This is no threat motherfucker, this is a promise. The ministry's days are numbered, oh one more thing.
Nikita changes into an exact duplicate of Falcon.
Falcon :
(In Pain)
You... won't pass.... as me... little girl.
Nikita :
(As Falcon)
Oh I will fuck boy, time for your nap.
She shoots him twice in the head, spraying blood, skull and brain matter all over the walls, she picks up his body and stuffs it under the seat, luckily the blood matches the carpet. She holsters her gun and takes his clothes, walking out. One of the other members Heartbreak comes over to him, he brushes him off and gives him a piece of paper with a new account number. He gives him a " keep this quiet" look, he nods and Nikita heads out. She heads to a nearby alley and changes back.
She effortlessly vaults up the wall, and shudders. She uses her com link to contact William.
Nikita :
It's done, Falcons taking his nap. I've gave heartbreak the account number.
William Reed :
Excellent news white mist. Come home, and we'll discuss your next target

<u>End of Chapter Six</u>

Retaliation

The other members with Vandenberg are talking, when he raises his hand to silence them.
Director Vandenberg:
Gentlemen please. Though we mourn the death of Falcon, we must carry on. I propose we send tracker, to hunt down his assailant.
Heartbreak:
Send another failure? Out of the question. We will wait for them to come to us.
Tornado:
What then? Let them murder another one of us? I won't let that happen. Vandenberg! Contact tracker, bring him directly to us.
Director Vandenberg:
Yes sir.
He leaves them to squabble, as he heads into his office, locking the door. Pours himself a whisky and flops onto his couch. Swirling his drink, smiling smugly.
Director Vandenberg:
Computer, where is Tracker?
Computer Voice:
Current location is in a local bar. Opening com link.
The com link beeps as it connects.
Tracker:
What's up boss?
Director Vandenberg:
I need you to find the perpetrator, who killed Falcon.

Tracker:
You got it boss! Consider it done.
Director Vandenberg:
If you find any further information, I'll add a bonus.
Tracker:
Yes boss, loud and clear.
The com link cuts out and Vandenberg places his drink on the table, then takes a nap still smiling
***

Night begins to fall as the sun sets. We find Tracker in the local nightclub The Den. He sits in one of the booths, sipping a cold beer. We see Dr. Wagner enter looking nervous. Tracker flashes his cybernetic eye to catch his attention. He hurriedly walks over to the booth and sits.
Tracker:
Relax doc!
Dr. Wagner:
I hope William forgives me for this.
Tracker:
You need the money, and I've got the funds. You've got info, and I want it.
Dr. Wagner:
You sure they'll be no... repercussions.
Tracker:
(Lying)
Chill... doc. I swear they'll be no come back.
He snaps his fingers to get a nearby waitress to order a drink.
Dr. Wagner:

Normally I wouldn't be here, dealing with... people like you.

The waitress puts the drink on the table, Dr. Wagner looks at her, while he does tracker puts a substance in it, swirling it as it disappears.

Tracker:

I know a tweaker, when I see one. It's simple, you give what I want. And you get cash to get your next hit. I'll ask this once... who... killed... Falcon!

For several minutes there is deadly silence, all we hear dance music playing.

Dr. Wagner:

It was... Nikita!

Tracker:

(Laughs)

See, that wasn't so hard! Have a drink doc... you earned it.

He quickly grabs the glass and hungrily drinks. His nerves now gone, he relaxes a little. Suddenly he starts to struggle for breath, he glares at tracker who smiles.

Dr. Wagner:

(Laboured Breathing)

You... bastard....

Tracker:

Sorry doc, loose ends and all.

Dr. Wagner slumps hard onto the table dead. Tracker gets up, he heads out activating his com link.

Tracker:

Boss, I know who killed Falcon.... your former skilled assassin.

Vandenberg responds.:
Director Vandenberg

Silent knight... I knew it. Let me make this VERY clear. I... WANT... HER... DEAD!
Tracker
Consider it done, boss!
The com link cuts off as tracker exits the nightclub. And begins his hunt for silent knight.
After many hours searching, he finally tracks her down. He enters macs bar smiling. She clocks him, realising that he knows. But she fake smiles as he sits down.
Tracker:
Let's cut to the chase, you know why I'm here. Nothing personal.
Nikita:
Oh... I know...everything. let me guess, knowing the doc was... sniffing. You offered him cash for his habit. But Vandenberg told you to... tie up loose ends. So I thought you'd not shoot him, too messy. You had to be more... discreet. Poison in the drink act. Quick... painless!
Tracker:
(Slow Clapping)
Quite the blood hound. Here's the thing, we handle this in here, putting THEM in harms way... or outback one on one, no guns. Your choice!
Nikita smiles and suddenly roundhouse kicks him square in the jaw hard. Then grabs him and flings him violently through one of the windows. She runs out and yells to mac she will compensate him for the window. Tracker weakly gets back to his feet, turning to face her, wiping the glowing blood of his lips.
Tracker:

Your a tough one, nice kick. Shall we dance?

He runs towards her, somersaulting over her. Then knees her in the back hard, she yells in pain, stumbling then falls.

Her HUD displays spinal cord critical damage. Mobility reduced by 56%. Repair required urgently. Nikita struggles to stand. Tracker laughs hysterically.

Nikita

(In Pain)

Oh... I'm... I'm not done with you... lover.

Tracker :

Sweetheart... please...

Nikita rips out a nearby lamppost, smacking tracker violently with full force which launches him into a nearby building. He lands bone crunchingly hard. He shakes off his confusion to see Nikita struggling to reach him. He laughs again, as he rushes towards her, grabbing her by the arm and launches her into another building violently. He walks towards her as the dust clears. Sparks from her broken body are seen. Her face and body mangled, her eyes flicker as she fights to stay awake.

Tracker :

Poor little Nicky, played with the big boys... but lost. You put up a good fight.

He turns and walks away laughing. Nikita twitches and sparks from time to time.

Nikita :

S... Sa... Safe.... safeguard.

A blue light envelopes her and she fades into thin air.

End of Chapter Seven

New & Improved

Nikita is in a large circular tank, filled with blue water, she has tubes inserted in what's left of her torso, and a mask to aid her breathing. William is looking at her concerned as she sleeps.

Dr. Wagner :
(Metallic Voice)
Bedside vigil?
William Reed :
(Chuckles)
Something like that.
William turns to face Dr. Wagner who is a large metal spider like creature.
Dr. Wagner :
My... avatar was destroyed. Poisoned by tracker. She is doing well, old friend. Her recovery is top priority. Currently I'm working on a design, which will give tracker a run for his money. Also I will... redefine her systems. Giving her all the advantages I can give her.
William Reed :
Peter, my dear friend... words can't...
Dr. Wagner :
I know my friend... I know. You don't have to say anything, or worry. She's in safe hands. I will give her the best upgrades I can.
William Reed :

Even if I have to, access there databases I.....
Dr. Wagner:
No need, it's already done. It was to be a reward for that low life scum. But now it's ours. I've also deleted the schematics as well as corrupting the back up.
William and Peter smile, then he turns to Nikita.

***

Vandenberg is fuming with anger. He paces up and down his office.
Director Vandenberg:
Check it again.
Ministry Computer:
File not found, back up is corrupted. Unable to retrieve data.
Director Vandenberg:
FUCKING... CHECK IT AGAIN.
Ministry Computer:
Sir, I've checked and rechecked. The upgrade for tracker is no longer in the database. Clearly it has been downloaded and deleted, also the backup was corrupted to cover there tracks.
Director Vandenberg:
(Through clenched teeth)
William... that fucking bitch. He did this. Let me guess, no trace!
Ministry Computer:
Yes sir.
Director Vandenberg:
I fucking knew it. Where's that useless piece of shit?
Ministry Computer:
Repair centre, cosmetic surgery to his lower jaw.

Director Vandenberg:

Pause surgery, open vid com link.

A red screen pops up and crackles into life. We see a laser scalpel repairing trackers face but abruptly stops.

Tracker:

I'm busy!

Director Vandenberg:

Listen here, you vain fucktard... clearly you didn't finish the job. The bonus I... had for you is now in there hands. The file is gone, the backup corrupted.

Tracker:

(Uninterested)

So what, let them have there toy. Computer continue.

The scalpel fizzes into life as it continues to repair his face.

Director Vandenberg:

You fucking listen here, you asshole. I OWN YOU. Your MY bitch, I say jump... you say how high... got it?

Tracker:

(Laughing)

You think you own me shithead? I disarmed your, little gift in my head.. I'd be more nicer to me. You don't want the others, to find out what you did... dealers choice.

Director Vandenberg:

Those old fuckers, they don't scare...

A familiar voice butt's in.

Tornado:

(Emotionless)

Oh, really Samuel? We don't scare you? Tracker was delighted to inform us, of your... little side project. Secondly your back account is now frozen. Finally...

your fired, your personal effects will be incinerated. Good luck living on the streets.
The vid com link abruptly cuts off. Two robot security guards, force the doors open and aim there weapons at him. Signalling him to leave.

***

The blue water in the tank empties and the cylinder container fizzes open. Her eyes flutter, then snap open and dart in fear. Dr. Wagner appears reassuring her. She looks at him in horror. He smiles reassuringly at her.

Dr. Wagner:

Your safe my dear, apologies for my... appearance. It enables me to move quickly about the lab. Don't try to speak, your vocal chord box was damaged in your recent altercation.

Nikita:

(Struggling)

O...Out... long...

Dr. Wagner:

A few months, I had to place you in a medical induced stasis... your cybernetics were too badly damaged, your spinal column strut was heavily damaged. Repairs are being carried out. I've redefined your design, using specifications from there databases. Some good news, I'm constructing new cybernetics, and tweaking your targeting system. And increasing reaction time.

William enters the room to see Nikita awake, he smiles happily and relieved.

William Reed:

Good to see you awake my dear. How are you feeling.

Nikita:
(Forcing a smile)
P.... pe... peachy!
Dr. Wagner:
Her vitals are improving, reconstruction will commence soon.
Nikita:
N...no! D...do it... now... no.. arg... arguing.
William Reed:
Your not strong enough yet.
Dr. Wagner:
I agree with William.
Nikita:
T... tracker.... pay... payback. Don't... gi... give a... fuck... about.... p... pain.

William nods to Dr. Wagner who scurries off and pushes some buttons. Segments of the floor slide open to reveal sleek new cybernetics. Nikita nods as the new arms slam into the sockets, she screams in pain, but looks at them and shakes her head to say " don't stop". She screams even louder ad her new legs slam into her cybernetic/ organic stumps. They all lock into place. Finally a new gun is placed in her holster, as she passes out.

Dr. Wagner:
I'm... sorry!
William Reed:
Don't be... seal her up for her to...
Nikita:
(More Seductively)
Now why would you want yo do that?

She raises her head as her face instantly repairs itself.

End of Chapter 8

Showdown

Tracker is disposing his latest victim in a large trash compactor. He uses his com link to contact Vandenberg. But tornado picks up.
Tracker:
Where's the boss?
Tornado:
I will be overseeing your objectives, from now on. Vandenberg no longer works for us. The data from your altercation with our... former top assassin indicates that you left her alive. This will not be tolerated, sloppy work will simply not do....
Tracker:
I fucked her up bad, might be dead already. So relax... boss. Its handled.
Tornado:
Handled? HANDLED? YOUR ARROGANCE AND EGO, GOT IN THE WAY OF FINISHING YOUR MISSION... YOUR GOING TO FIND HER AND...
Suddenly we hear a very familiar voice.
Nikita:
Did you miss me... lover?
Tracker turns to see her. He cuts off the com link abruptly. Stunned but regains his composure.
Tracker:

I thought you were dead. Love the new look... but it won't stop me breaking you in half...
Nikita :

Lover, your teasing me... try as you might but you won't be able to... penetrate me with your... tiny... useless... knee piece.
Tracker :

I kicked your ass once, what makes you think I won't do it again....
Nikita :

Let's cut the shut, shall we?

Nikita moves fluidly and quickly, grabs tracker and hurtles him into a nearby trash bin. A loud clang is heard as it rips in half like paper. He crashes violently into the wall. He awkwardly picks himself up, stumbling to walk. He draws his guns and fires. Nikita easily dodges them so fast she ricochets them back at him. They instantly hit him in his leg struts. His legs collapse underneath him. Nikita stands there looking over him.

He drags himself out the large hole in the wall. His legs catch on metal beams, ripping them clean off. Sparks fly and glowing blood spurts out as he crawls to a nearby street lamp, leaning against it.
Tracker :

(Laughing Through Pain)

Your a tough bitch, I'll give... you that. But this... ain't over...

Tracker disappears in a white light. Nikita sighs in frustration.
Nikita :

A (Chuckles)
You clever motherfucker, next time. Next time.
We watch as she runs off, running up along the rooftops. We slowly turn to see someone watching her, all we see are glowing gold eyes.

www.ingramcontent.com/pod-product-compliance
Lightning Source LLC
LaVergne TN
LVHW041558070526
838199LV00046B/2029